to the Sunday
School of
Park St. Church

from

Faye Gilmour

November 1999

B254 © APCo

Also by Nick Butterworth and Mick Inkpen:

The House on the Rock, The Lost Sheep,
The Two Sons, The Precious Pearl,
The Magpie's Story, The Mouse's Story,
The Fox's Story, The Cat's Story.

Marshall Morgan and Scott
Marshall Pickering
34 − 42 Cleveland Street, London, W1P 5FB, U.K.

Copyright © 1989 Nick Butterworth & Mick Inkpen
First published in 1989 by Marshall Morgan and Scott Publications Ltd
Part of the Marshall Pickering Holdings Group

A subsidiary of the Zondervan Corporation

First published in the USA by
Zondervan Publishing House, 1415 Lake Drive, S.E.,
Grand Rapids, Michigan 49506

British Library CIP Data
Butterworth, Nick
  Ten silver coins
  1. Bible. N.T. Parables: Lost piece of silver
  − stories for children
  I. Title   II. Inkpen, Mick   III. Series
  226'.8

  cat. # 19105
  ISBN 0−310−55950−2

Printed and bound in Italy

The Ten Silver Coins

Nick Butterworth and Mick Inkpen

Zondervan Publishing House
Grand Rapids, Michigan

Here is a woman. She has ten silver coins. She likes to count them.

One, two, three, four...

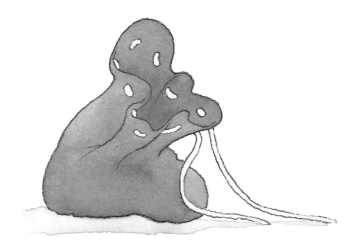

Oops! Silly cat! Now they've gone all over the place.

The woman picks up her silver coins. They have been scattered everywhere!

The cat doesn't care. He has stretched out and gone to sleep.

The woman counts her silver coins again. But there are only nine. One of them is missing!

Never mind, it can't have gone far.

Perhaps it is under the rug.
No. There is no sign of it there.

Perhaps it has bounced into the fireplace. Carefully she sifts through the ashes.

What a messy job! But no, there is no coin.

Perhaps it rolled right under the door and out into the garden.

She searches and searches, but she cannot find the coin anywhere.

She even looks inside her
pots and pans, even though she
really knows it can't be there.

Clatter! Bang! What a noise
she is making!

She's making so much noise, she wakes up the cat. Serves him right. He's off to find a quiet spot in the garden.

There it is! The cat was lying on it all the time! The missing silver coin is found!

The woman laughs. She is so
happy she calls a friend to
tell her the good news.

Jesus says, "We are like the woman's silver coins. God wants every single one of us."